Giving-
Tithing & Offerings
(Principle and Standard)

4th Edition
Revised and Expanded

By
REV. PETER KOFI NYARKOH

Revised and Expanded 2020
ISBN: 978-9988-53-579-7

Unless otherwise stated scripture quotations are from
THE GOOD NEWS TRANSLATION

Publish by:
ERC Publication,
P.O. Box KS 10095,
Kumasi.

Cell Phone: +233 (0) 208170193, +233 (0) 243148383

Cover Design by:
DP Solutions Ghana
+233 (0) 24 595 9796

For more copies contact:
EVANGELISM RESOURCE CENTRE (ERC)
AND PETERGRACE VENTURES
P. O. BOX KS 10095 KUMASI

(Lead a Bible Study Life that is an Application of Bible Truth)

Dedication

All Bible Study Leaders and my Grandchildren I love you.

Acknowledgments

I humbly express my sincere appreciation to the hundreds of people who took time to use the manuscripts during their congregational Bible Studies. Without their help this book could not have been published.

Special thanks to Rev. Rose B. Puplampu who computerized the scripts and did the final proof-reading. Also to Mrs. Afua Konadu Nyarkoh Mensah I say thank you for the final proof-reading.

Finally, I want to thank Mama Grace and all my grandchildren for their love and support which enable me to complete this 4th edition.

God bless you all.

Table Of Contents

Resources By The Same Author

1. The Presbyters' Handbook (Elders & Leaders' Guide)

Preaching Skills and Pulpit Manners (The Preacher's Manual)

3. New Members Class Study Guide (Procedures for Admission of New Members)

4. Children's Ministry -The Unfinished Task (Handbook for Children Service Teachers)

5. Pastors' Companion- (The Pastor's Manual)

6. Bible Study Made Simple (Taking the Lid off Bible Study)

7. Marriage Counselling Handbook (Regulations, Practices and Procedures of a Progressive Christian Marriage)

8. Good News for Marriage Counselling Committee (A Comprehensive Guide)

9. The Choice? Life Partner (Pre-Marriage Counselling Handbook)

10. The Power of the Word and Prayer (Healing and Deliverance Made Simple)

11. Increasing Church Membership (A Task with a Vision Makes a Missionary)

12. Church Committees (Return To Dynamic Church Leadership)

13. Family Handbook (Procedures for Church Family)

14. The Health of the Church (Factors & Obstacles of Church Growth)

Leader's Guidelines

a. WHAT IS BIBLE STUDY?

Bible Study is to know Christ and make Him known and becoming like Him in attitudes, thoughts, speeches, actions and values. Its main purpose is application but not interpretation. It is the searching into God's word and applying the Truth learnt to one's daily life.

Bible Study is a life to be lived. It is an attempt to establish an intimate two-way communication with God. Never study the Bible with the attitude of finding a kind of truth that no one has ever known or finding truths to impress others. Try to get the most spiritual blessing from your Bible Study. Do not worry about what you do not understand when you study the Bible, rather worry about what you do understand but do not live by or apply it. (Extract from: Bible Study Made Simple by Rev. Peter Kofi Nyarkoh)

b. WHY MEMORIZE BIBLE VERSES?

We need to memorize portions of scripture for the following reasons:

1. Love for Christ
2. God's command (Deut. 11: 18 – 20)
3. An act with blessings (Jos. 1:8)
4. A witnessing tool (1Pet.3:15)
5. A weapon against worldliness, sins, Satan and temptation (Psalm 119:11; Matt. 4:4)
6. It provides peace of mind and heart (Ps. 119: 105)
7. It makes God's power available.

c. MEMORY VERSES

i. WHAT IS A BLOCK MEMORY VERSE?

This is a particular memory verse that runs through a set of lessons. That is, one memory verse is used for two or more lessons.

ii. ***WHAT IS A LESSON BY LESSON MEMORY VERSE?***

This is where each lesson or chapter has a memory verse.

d. HOW TO TEACH A MEMORY VERSE

1. Read the verse carefully.
2. Make sure you understand it and explain it to your group members.

   Know how it applies to the topic for study.
4. Divide the verse into natural phrases.
5. Begin by repeating the reference.
6. Then repeat the first phrase until the group knows it.
7. Repeat the reference and the first phrase till the group knows the two.
8. Add another phrase, till you come to the end of the natural phrases.
9. Repeat it several times till the group knows it
10. Repeat the whole verse with the reference.
11. Review is essential – as many times as the group meets.

Note:

Learn the memory verse at the beginning of the study. It is highly recommended.

b. Choose one translation. (Paraphrase Translations are not helpful in memorizing).

e. ORDER FOR A CONGREGATIONAL BIBLE STUDY

1. Signature hymn or song*
2. Opening prayer
3. Greetings and welcoming of members

Review of previous memory verse

5. Signature hymn or song* (where grouping is possible)
6. Read the passage for the day
7. Study and discussion
8. Summary and closing prayer
9. Signature hymn or song

**Signature Hymn/Song – it is a specific hymn/song chosen for introducing the lesson; it is sung while members are grouping for their studies and returning to their seats after studies.*

Lesson 1 | Who Are We?

READ

I Cor. 3:9

"For we are partners working together for God, and you are God's field. You are also God's building"

STUDY

Christ's giving of Himself for our salvation is the strongest example of ***Giving.*** As partners with God it is important for us to understand where responsibilities lie. Christians work together as ***partners*** who belong to God. Christians are God's ***field*** and God's ***building.*** Christ's work connects many different individuals, with variety of talents, gifts and abilities. Christians are in God's team performing special roles, thus making Christian useful members and not super members. Talent or Gift is the *unusual ability to do something well.* It can be developed by training and constant use. It is an exceptional ability, capability, skill, aptitude and endowment.

DISCUSSIONS:

1. How do you understand 1Cor.3:9?
   Who are the partners in this text?
3. Who are referred to in I Cor. 3:9 as God's field?
4. In what ways can a Christian work together with God as a:
   i. Partner
   ii. Field
5. Are you God's Building? How? Give Practical Examples

FACTS TO REMEMBER

Christians work together with God as partners. A Christian is God's field and God's building. Christians do not work on their own.

Lesson 2 | Surrendering To God

READ

1 Chron. 29:14 "Yet my people and I cannot really give you anything, because everything is a gift from you, and we have only given back what is yours already."

STUDY

Despite the above text many Christians still struggle to ***Give***. Some Christians ***Give*** willingly and cheerfully and in so doing submit to the authority of Christ. Other Christians ***Give*** alright, but do not give in accordance with the path of giving. But the action that releases a believer into the full blessings of God is total ***Surrender or Obedience*** – *unreserved submission of one's entire life, possession and plans to God's will and purpose.* Christians should allow God to have total control over their entire lives.

DISCUSSIONS:

What releases God's blessing?

2. What is total Surrender?

Explain the word "Obedience "in your own words.

4. In what ways can Christians Surrender to the:
    a. Plan of God (*intention of God for you achieve something)*
    b. Will of God *(sovereign control)*
    c. Purpose of God *(happenings that have being ordained by God)*

For example - in terms of: *Time, money, possession, marriage, work, children, family service to the church, etc.*

FACTS TO REMEMBER:

Everything you possess is given to you as a gift from God. Surrendering back to God everything in total obedience releases blessings

Lesson 3 | We Are Owner-Stewards

READ

Psalm 24:1

"The world and all that is in it belong to the Lord; the earth and all who live on it are his."

James 1:17 "Every good gift and every perfect present comes from heaven; it comes down from God, the Creator of the heavenly lights, who does not change or cause darkness by turning."

STUDY

A Steward takes care, administrates, and monitors what belong to someone else. Since God is the one who gives every physical and spiritual blessing, we must acknowledge His ownership and use these blessings to His glory and honour.

Every Christian is a Steward of everything he/she possesses. Christians are ***owner-stewards*** which means that *they own whatever God has given them and at the same time taking care of it for God.* They can use whatever God has given them to better their lives as well as the lives of others while keeping the principles of stewardship in mind.

It is only when we give ourselves to Jesus Christ that we learn what it means to ***Give*** our possessions (like: money, talents, experiences etc.), God has given us to support His work.

DISCUSSIONS:

1. How do you understand an Owner-Steward?
2. From the passages, are you an owner or a steward? Give reasons for your answer.
3. How many Stewards in your church do you know?
4. In What way(s) can we acknowledge God's ownership in our lives?

FACTS TO REMEMBER

We are stewards and not owners. Everything we have and own belongs to God. We can use whatever God gives us to better our lives and that of others to God's glory.

Lesson 4 | We Are Owner–Managers

READ

I Peter 4:10 "Each one, as a good manager of God's different gifts, must use for the good of others the special gift he has received from God."

b. I Cor. 4:1-2 "You should think of us as Christ's servants, who have been put in charge of God's secret truths. The one thing required of such servants (manager) is that they be faithful to their master."

STUDY

An Owner is the one to whom property belongs and has the legal or rightful title. A manager leads and controls resources given to him/her to the expected end or results. He/she administrates and monitors what belong to someone else. Since God is the (*Owner*) one who gives everything we have, we must acknowledge His ownership and accept the fact that we are not owners, but managers. God owns everything and we have an obligation to be faithful in our managerial duties. Christians are *Owner-Mangers* which means that, although, they possess whatever God has given them, they are managing it for God. They can control whatever God has given them to better their lives and that of others while keeping the principles of management in mind.

The Lord holds us accountable for the special responsibility of managing and taking care of the things He has given us. When we understand this *Owner-Manager* relationship that we enjoy with God's property, then it becomes easy to give. God expects us to be *faithful, surrender totally, hardworking and be diligent in the use of our minds, wisdom and intelligence.*

DISCUSSIONS:

1. How do you understand I Cor. 4:2?
2. What is the resources God has given to you? How are you managing them?
3. How do you understand Owner-Manager relationship with God?
4. What is accountability in the light of what God has given to you?

FACTS TO REMEMBER

Christians are Owner-Managers. They control what belongs to God. They can use their possession to better their lives and that of others for God's glory. God experts us to be faithful, diligent and surrender totally to Him

Lesson 5 | Giving As A Practice And A Standard

READ

Deut. 16:16-17 "All the men of your nation are to come to worship the LORD three times a year at the one place of worship: at Passover, Harvest Festival, and the Festival of Shelters. Each man is to bring a gift as he is able, in proportion to the blessings that the LORD your God has given him."

STUDY

Giving is a principle in the Bible, for God Himself gave His only son to the world. ***Giving*** sets models for ***Tithing and Offerings*** in an organized manner. ***Tithing and Offerings*** are the practice and standard of ***Giving.*** God has not changed and His principles are for all times. As people and society change, we need to search constantly for the ways and methods to apply the principles of God to our present circumstances. God is the same in Old Testament as He is today and will be forever. (*Heb.13:8 -"Jesus Christ is the same yesterday, today, and forever."*)

1. ***We must begin with Ten percent (10%)***

God expects us to give, and to begin with a percentage. In the Old Testament the law is ten percent (**10%**) however, in the New Testament it is more than 10% because of Grace, (note grace is more abundant).

Mal. 3:10 "Bring the full amount of your ***Tithes*** to the Temple, so that there will be plenty of food there. Put me to the test and you will see that I will open the windows of heaven and pour out on you in abundance all kinds of good things."

2. ***Everybody must give in proportion to whatever he/she receives or how God has blessed the person.***

1 Cor. 16:2 "Every Sunday each of you must put aside some money, in ***Proportion*** to what you have earned, and save it up, so that there will be no need to collect money when I come".

3. ***We are to give the first and best to the Lord.***

Prov. 3:9 "Honor the LORD by making him an offering from the ***Best*** of all that your land produces."

Give Always.

Deut. 14:23 "Then go to the one place where the LORD your God has chosen to be worshiped; and there in his presence eat the tithes of your grain, wine, and olive oil, and the first-born of your cattle and sheep. Do this so that you may learn to honour the LORD your God ***Always.***"

Give on Daily basis.

Num. 28:3-4 "These are the food offerings that are to be presented to the ***LORD***: for the ***Daily*** burnt offering, two one-year-old male lambs without any defects. Offer the first lamb in the morning, and the second in the evening."

Give Every Sunday (Weekly).

a. 1 Cor. 16:2 "***Every Sunday*** each of you must put aside some money, in proportion to what you have and save it up, so that there will be no need to collect money when I come."

b. Num. 28:9-10 "On the ***Sabbath Day*** offer two one- year-old male lambs without any defects, 4 pounds of flour mixed with olive oil as a grain offering, and the wine offering. This burnt offering is to be offered every ***Sabbath*** in addition to the daily offering with its wine offering".

7. ***Give Monthly.***

Num. 28:11 "Present a burnt offering to the LORD at the beginning of ***Each Month.***"

8. **Give *Yearly (Also Seasonally)***

Deut. 14:22 "Set aside a tithe—a tenth of all that your fields produce ***Each Year.***"

Give beyond your regular giving.

a. Acts 4:34-35 "There was no one in the group who was in need. ***Those Who Owned Fields Or Houses Would Sell Them,*** bring the money received from the sale, and turn it over to the apostles; and the money was distributed according to the needs of the people."

10. Give according to your Earning structures or arrangements.

1 Cor. 16:2 "Every Sunday each of you must put aside some money, in

proportion to what you have ***Earned,*** and save it up, so that there will be no need to collect money when I come."

DISCUSSIONS:

1. Mention 4 of the practices and standards in ***Giving***? Are these in your congregation?
2. Has God changed in His principle of ***Giving?*** Yes or No, explain your answer.

   How can you relate Heb. 13:8 to God's principles of giving?
4. Do you think change in society can change the application of God's principle of ***Giving*** by Christians? Explain.

FACTS TO REMEMBER

The principle of ***Giving*** as outlined in the Bible has not change because God Himself has not changed.

Lesson 6 | What Is Tithe?

READ

a. ***Mal 3:10 "Bring the full amount of your tithes to the Temple, so that there will be plenty of food there. Put me to the test and you will see that I will open the windows of heaven and pour out on you in abundance all kinds of good things."***
b. ***Hebrews 7:2a "And Abraham gave him one tenth of all he had taken."***

STUDY

Tithe is a fixed amount of money or goods that is given regularly in order to support God's work, His people and charity. A tenth of the whole collection, set aside for God or a tenth of what one earns and receives as gifts. Tithe is a practice and standard of ***Giving.*** In ***Tithing,*** you look at what God has given you, what God can give to you and what you can give God in appreciation.

Tithe is not restricted to agricultural products alone, it includes cash and kind, experiences, skills and talents among others.
Tithing opens the door for one to escape from poverty , lack and curses to your wealthy place.

DISCUSSIONS:

What is ***Tithe*** in your own words?
2. Should gifts be ***Tithed***? Discuss
3. If you want to escape from lack or poverty, what should you do according to lesson 6?
4. What percentage of my earnings and gifts can I give as a ***Tithe***?

FACTS TO REMEMBER

Tithe is a tenth of what one earns and receives as gifts. In ***Tithing,*** consider what God has given you, what He can give and what you can give as an appreciation.

NB: Giving is a principle in the Bible and tithing is a practice and a standard of ***Giving.***

Lesson 7 | Origin Of Tithe?

READAD

Gen 14:20b "And Abram gave Melchizedek a Tenth of all the loot he had recovered."

b. ***Gen 28:22 "This memorial stone which I have set up will be the place where you are worshiped, and I will give you a Tenth of everything you give me."***

c. ***Heb. 7: 2 "And Abraham gave him one Tenth of all he had taken."***

d. ***Heb. 7:6 "Melchizedek was not descended from Levi, but he collected one tenth from Abraham and blessed him, the man who received God's promises "***

STUDY

Several centuries before the law was given on Mount Sinai, Abram gave a tithe to Melchizedek a representative of God. This is the first time ***Tithe*** is mentioned in the Bible. Long before ***Tithe*** became the Levitical Order, there existed Melchizedek Order. Jacob promised to give a ***Tenth*** of all that GOD will bless him with as he pledged his future to God.

Note: Levitical order is where tithe was paid to the Levite. Melchizedek Order is where ***Tithe*** was paid to Melchizedek and this was the original order. (Read Hebrews 7:1-10)

DISCUSSIONS:

When did ***Tithing*** start?

2. Who first gave ***Tithe*** and to whom?
3. Jacob promised to give to God, how much of his increase?
4. How do you understand Levitical and Melchizedek orders.

FACTS TO REMEMBER

The first recorded ***Tithe*** was paid by Abram to Melchizedek. ***Tithe*** exited before the law was given on Mount Sinai.

Lesson 8 | What Is Offering?

READ

2 Chron. 31:3 "From his own flocks and herds he provided animals for the burnt offerings each morning and evening, and for those offered on the Sabbath, at the New Moon Festival, and at the other festivals which are required by the Law of the LORD."

b. ***Neh. 10:33 "We will provide for the Temple worship the following: the sacred bread, the daily grain offering, the animals to be burned each day as sacrifices, the sacred offerings for Sabbaths, New Moon Festivals, and other festivals, the other sacred offerings, the offerings to take away the sins of Israel, and anything else needed for the Temple."***

STUDY

Offering is a gift, a tribute or a sacrifice, which is given to God. A Gift is something given willingly to someone without payment, to show appreciation. A Gift is a free will offer and not forced or required. It is normally given without expectation or a payback in future.

Tribute, on the hand, is a required payment owed to a higher authority or a payment made periodically by one ruler to another, as a sign of dependence.

Sacrifice is surrendering or giving up something of value in obedience to God without any expectation. You are your ***Offering***, for the giver is one with what he/she offers. Your ***Offering*** defines your relationship with God. Give to God as you think He is.

DISCUSSIONS:

1. What is ***Offering***?
2. In what forms can we give ***Offering*** to God. Name and explain
3. How can an ***Offering*** define the giver's relationship with God?

FACTS TO REMEMBER

Offering comes as a gift, a tribute or a sacrifice. Your ***Offering*** defines your relationship with God. Give to God as you think He is.

Lesson 9 | Types Of Offering 1

INTRODUCTION TO LESSONS 9 TO 12

God commanded Moses to tell the people of Israel to observe constantly the set times for festivals. During such periods they were to offer specific offerings to God. The import and the application of what God said to the people of Israel in the Old Testament differ in many respects to the Christians of today in terms of application. Let us understand what God told the people of Israel and identify the portions that Christians of today can apply and how to do them. There are records in the Bible which gave clear indication that Jesus and the Apostles as well and the New Testament church kept some holy festivals – Matt 26:2,17-19; Mark 14:12-16 etc. The festivals were descriptions of events of people of the Old Testament. These descriptions are not intended by God to be prescriptions for Christians of today to make decisions and choices on. For instance: Abraham and the sacrifice of Isaac – is a description of his life and commitment to God, but not a prescription for the church of today to follow to sacrifice human beings. However, the significance here is Abraham's willingness and obedience to give his son. This is to point to us our willingness and obedience to offer to God. God's principle for giving has not change but the practices and standards do change. Your church services become an opportunity to ***Offer*** to support God's work. Therefore, at all church activities and meetings, opportunities will be created for you to ***Offer*** to support God's work. The Church's events are your opportunity to contribute to support the church's ministry.

FIRST FRUITS OFFERING
(***Obligation to everyone***)

READ

- *a.* ***Numbers 18:12 –"I am giving you all the best of the first produce which the Israelites give me each year: olive oil, wine, and grain."***
- *b.* ***Deut. 26:2,10 – "each of you must place in a basket the first part of each crop that you harvest and you must take it with you to the one place of worship... So now I bring to the LORD the first part of the harvest that He has given me.' "Then set the basket down in the***

LORD's presence and worship there."

c. ***Gen. 4: 4 – "But Abel brought fat portions from some of the firstborn of his flock. The Lord looked with favor on Abel and his offering," NIV***
d. ***Other Supporting verses – Exodus 13:2; Gen.4:1-7***

STUDY

First fruit ***Offering*** means ***Offering*** to God your first and foremost, top or maiden product of your labour or work. Such an ***Offering*** is done before any other thing is considered and cuts across all categories of work, profession and persons. First fruits are ***Offered*** as a sign of acknowledging the lordship of God and his provision for our lives, expressing our dependence and trust in Him.

Genesis 4:1-5 recorded the first ***Offering*** given by humankind to God. In this ***Offering*** the acts of Abel gave a clear principle to be followed by all. Abel brought fat portions of the firstborn of his flock. Out of his toils, Abel ***Offered*** his first fruit to God which the Lord was pleased with.

This ***Offering*** established a level of identity and relationship with God giving the indication that Abel identify with his ***Offering***.

Offer to God your first fruit from the reward of your labour and your earnings, be it your allowances, salaries, remunerations, interest on investments, profits among others.

DISCUSSIONS:

1. Describe Abel's first ***Offering***. What can we learn from it?
2. In what way can we establish a relationship with God through our first fruit ***Offering***?
3. Name some of the rewards or produces from which you can offer first fruit to God.
4. Why do we ***Offer*** our first fruit to God?

FACTS TO REMEMBER

First fruit ***Offering*** is the ***Offering*** of first and foremost reward, and product of our labour to God. It is done to acknowledge the Lordship and provision of God over our lives

Lesson 10 | Types Of Offering 2

STUDY:
DEMANDED OFFERING

Genesis 22:2 – "He said, "Take your son, your only son Isaac, whom you love, and go to the land of Moriah, and offer him there as a burnt offering on one of the mountains of which I shall tell you." ESV.

Demanded ***Offering*** is an ***Offering*** required by God, it demands specific items and quality. In such ***Offering***, God decides what one is expected to bring as ***Offering***. God said to Abraham go and sacrifice your son Isaac. That is, all that Abraham had and the carrier of the Promise of God. This is neither first fruit nor ***Tithe***, but a special ***Offering*** demanded by God from Abraham. It can also be referred to as a test ***Offering***.

1. **PERSONAL VOW OR COVENANT OFFERING**
   Judges 11:30-31,39 – "And Jephthah made a vow to the Lord: "If you give the Ammonites into my hands, 31 whatever comes out of the door of my house to meet me when I return in triumph from the Ammonites will be the Lord's, and I will sacrifice it as a burnt offering... After the two months, she returned to her father and he did to her as he had vowed. And she was a virgin. NIV

b. ***Num. 30:2 "When a man makes a vow to give something to the LORD or takes an oath to abstain from something, he must not break his promise, but must do everything that he said he would."***

c. ***Gen 28:20-21 "Then Jacob made a vow to the LORD: "If you will be with me and protect me on the journey I am making and give me food and clothing, and if I return safely to my father's home, then you will be my God."***

d. ***Others supporting Verses: Deut. 23:21-23; Exo 22:29-31; Eccl 5:4-7***
   Personal vow/covenant ***Offering*** is an irrevocable agreement with God. It is a solemn serious and sacred promise/pledge to do something, perform an act or behave in a particular manner when a request to God has been fulfilled.

2. **FELLOWSHIP, FREEWILL OR VOLUNTARY OFFERING**

Lev. 22:21 – "when anyone presents a fellowship offering to the LORD, whether as fulfilment of a vow or as a freewill offering, the animal must be without any defects if it is to be accepted."

b. ***Ezra 3:5 – "the offerings that were given to the LORD voluntarily."***

c. ***Genesis 8:20 – "Then Noah built an altar to the Lord and took some of every clean animal and some of every clean bird and offered burnt offerings on the altar".***

Fellowship, Freewill or voluntary ***Offering*** is an ***Offering*** done willingly at the person's own choice, as an appreciation to God. It is a gift and sacrifice ***Offering***. It is neither demanded nor required. It is offered out of what God had preserved. You may have suffered and as a result, lost a lot of possession but out of what God has preserved you ***Offer*** a freewill or voluntary ***Offering*** as in the case of Noah. This is to show gratitude – saying Lord, this is what is in my hands, I am grateful. In such ***Offering*** bring that which is clean, of value and significant to honour God. Freewill or voluntary offering affairs our trust in God and give us assurance of His protection for generations yet unborn. Noah's ***Offering*** after the flood attracted a promise of protection for future generation from God. (Gen. 8:21)

3. **OFFERINGS AT SPECIFIC TIMES/PERIODS**

Read Numbers 28

Numbers 28 outlines some specific times or periods at which God commanded the people of Israel to offer to Him. These are:

a. **DAILY:**

vs.3 – "These are the food offerings that are to be presented to the Lord: for the daily burnt offering, two one-year-old male lambs without any defects."

b. **WEEKLY (SABBATH OFFERING):**

vs. 9-10 – On the Sabbath day offer two one-year-old male lambs without any defects, 4 pounds of flour mixed with olive oil as a grain offering, and the wine offering. 10 This burnt offering is to be offered every Sabbath in addition to the daily offering with its wine offering.

c. MONTHLY:

d. *vs 11-15 – "Present a burnt offering to the Lord at the beginning of each month ... This is the regulation for the burnt offering for the first day of each month throughout the year... "*

e. ANNUALLY:

vs 16-25 – "The Passover Festival in honor of the Lord is to be held on the fourteenth day of the first month ... The Passover Festival in honor of the Lord is to be held on the fourteenth day of the first month"

4. SPECIAL OFFERINGS

These are ***Offerings*** given for particular purposes. They are different from the usual way a person gives in the Church and are clearly defined offerings.

Members Offer to Support Church Projects and Events.

Neh. 7:70-72 – *Many of the people contributed to help pay the cost of restoring the Temple:*

- The governor: 270 ounces of gold, 50 ceremonial bowls and 530 robes for priests
- Heads of clans: 337 pounds of gold and 3, 215 pounds of silver.
- The rest of the people: 337 pounds of gold, 2,923 pounds of silver and 67 robes for priests.

b. Leaders Offer For The Dedication

Num. 7:10-11 – *"The leaders also brought offerings to celebrate the dedication of the altar. When they were ready to present their gifts at the altar, the LORD said to Moses, "Tell them that each day for a period of twelve days one of the leaders is to present his gifts for the dedication of the altar."*

c. Officials offer to support the work of the Temple

1 Chron. 29:6-8 – "Then the heads of the clans, the officials of the tribes, the commanders of the army, and the administrators of the royal property volunteered to give the following for the work on the Temple: 190 tons of gold, 380 tons of silver, 675 tons of bronze and 3,750 tons of iron. Those who had precious stones gave them to the Temple treasury, which was administered by

Jehiel of the Levite clan of Gershon."

DISCUSSIONS:

1. According to Numbers 28, at what set times are we required to ***Offer*** to the Lord?

   Explain the following in your own words:
   i. Demanded **Offering**
   ii. Freewill **Offering**
   iii. Special **Offering**
3. How do you understand Personal Vow ***Offering?*** What lessons can you learn from Jephthah's experience?
4. From this study, is it required to give ***offering(s)*** to the Lord after paying your ***Tithe***? Explain your answer.

FACTS TO REMEMBER

Aside our regular ***Offerings***, God demands specific ***Offerings*** from His people. Also there are specific times at which we are expected to ***Offer*** such as – daily, weekly, monthly and yearly. Offerings to God can also be through a personal vow, freewill offering or special ***Offering***.

Lesson 11 | Types Of Offering 3

STUDY

1. TITHE OF TITHE

This is the payment of a tenth of all ***Tithes.*** When a person pays a ***Tenth*** of a tithe paid to him/her is referred to as ***Tithe of Tithe***. This basically relates to Priests or persons who receive ***Tithes*** from others. The Lord required that the Priests present ***Offering*** to Him from all the tithes they received from the Israelites.

a. ***Num.18:26 – "Moreover, you shall speak and say to the Levites, 'When you take from the people of Israel the tithe that I have given you from them for your inheritance, then you shall present a contribution from it to the Lord, a tithe of the tithe." ESV***
b. ***Neh. 10:38 "Priests who are descended from Aaron are to be with the Levites when tithes are collected, and for use in the Temple the Levites are to take to the Temple storerooms one-tenth of all the tithes they collect".***

2. OFFERINGS FOR THE POOR, WIDOW, ORPHAN AND ALIEN (CHARITY)

These are ***Offerings*** voluntarily given in kind or cash to support the needy for their well-being. For the promotion of people's welfare members ***Offer*** willingly to support.

Deut. 15:10-11 "Give to them freely and unselfishly, and the LORD will bless you in everything you do. There will always be some Israelites who are poor and in need, and so I command you to be generous to them."

b. ***Deut. 14:29 "this food is for the Levites, since they own no property, and for the foreigners, orphans, and widows who live in your towns. They are to come and get all they need. Do this, and the LORD your God will bless you in everything you do."***

3. **OFFERING AT THE NEW MOONS**

   a. ***New Moon Festivals-*** *Neh.10:33c – "for the offerings on the Sabbaths, New Moon festivals and appointed feasts; for the holy offerings;"* NIV

      2Chron.2:4b – "It will be a holy place where my people and I will worship him by burning incense of fragrant spices, where we will present offerings of sacred bread to him continuously, and where we will offer burnt offerings every morning and evening, as well as on Sabbaths, New Moon Festivals, and other holy days honoring the Lord our God."

4. ***Wood Offering***

   Remember all this, O God, and give me credit for it:

   a. *Neh.10:34 "We, the people, priests, and Levites, will draw lots each year to determine which clans are to provide wood to burn the sacrifices offered to the LORD our God, according to the requirements of the Law."*
   b. *Neh. 13:31 "I arranged for the wood used for burning the offerings to be brought at the proper times, and for the people to bring their offerings of the first grain and the first fruits that ripened. Remember all this, O God, and give me credit for it."*

DISCUSSIONS:

1. Explain in your own words how you understand "***Tithe of Tithe"***
2. In what ways can we support the poor, widows, orphans and aliens among us?
3. How can we apply Nehemiah 10:34 in our day to day Christian life?
4. Do people give voluntarily to their church? How?

FACTS TO REMEMBER

required by the Lord to pay a tenth of all **Tithes** collected. It is our obligation as a church to support the poor, widows, orphans and aliens among us. Families within the church may provide for specific needs of the church as their support for the church's ministry.

Lesson 12 | Tithing And Offerings In The New Testament 1

READ

Mat. 23:23 – "Woe to you, teachers of the law and Pharisees, you hypocrites! You give a tenth of your spices—mint, dill and cumin. But you have neglected the more important matters of the law—justice, mercy and faithfulness. You should have practiced the latter, without neglecting the former."

STUDY

The earthly ministry of our Lord Jesus Christ was supported by many people financially. The Christian Church of today also needs to be supported financially. Throughout the New Testament, Jesus Christ and the disciples used money to pay bills and all other expenses. It is therefore not wrong for the church of today to use money to cater for their financial requirements. Jesus made it clear that He did not come to abolish the law or the prophets but He came to fulfil them (Matt. 5 17). Jesus said we should not neglect the tithe rather we should add to it justice, mercy and faithfulness. ***Tithe*** did not cease in the New Testament, we can do it and do it better. ***Giving – tithing and offerings*** should not be understood as Old Testament law but a Christian obligation.

The God of the Old Testament is the same God of the New Testament, the same for ever and ever. The God of Abraham and the God of Christians is the same God. All the principles of God are eternal, but note, the practices and standards do change periodically depending on the situation and circumstances. ***Giving*** as a principle has not changed and it remains the same; tithing and ***Offering*** as practices and standards have changed with time due to the changes in people's conditions and situation. God does not change or improve His Word, Principles and Values.

DISCUSSIONS:

1. Did ***Tithe*** cease in the New Testament? Explain your answer.
2. How do you understand Matt 23:23
3. What is Jesus' requirement on payment of ***Tithes*** and ***Offerings***?
4. In what ways can we fulfil Jesus' requirement on ***Tithes*** and ***Offerings***?

FACTS TO REMEMBER

Jesus did not come to abolish the law but He came to fulfil them. Jesus did not abolish ***Tithing*** in the New Testament times rather He added to it. He required that justice, mercy and faithfulness must prevail among us while we keep ***Tithing***. The God of the Old Testament is the same God of the New Testament.

Lesson 13 | Tithing And Offering In The New Testament 2

READ

ACTS 4:32-37

"All the believers were one in heart and mind. No one claimed that any of his possessions was his own, but they shared everything they had. 33 With great power the apostles continued to testify to the resurrection of the Lord Jesus, and much grace was upon them all. 34 There were no needy persons among them. For from time to time those who owned lands or houses sold them, brought the money from the sales 35 and put it at the apostles' feet, and it was distributed to anyone as he had need. 36 Joseph, a Levite from Cyprus, whom the apostles called Barnabas (which means Son of Encouragement), 37 sold a field he owned and brought the money and put it at the apostles' feet." NIV

STUDY

The first detailed recorded account on giving of ***Offering*** in the New Testament is in Acts 4:32-37. This is a clear Spirit of ***Giving*** in the New Testament Church.

1. All the believers were one in heart and mind, (***a church where Unity prevails***).
2. No one claimed that any of their possessions was their own, (***they are Stewards***)
3. All believers shared everything they had, (a ***sharing Church***)
4. Those who owned land or houses sold them, brought the money from the sales and put it at the Apostles' feet, (***they gave up their wealth to the Church***).
5. The Levite Barnabas sold a field he owned and brought the money and put it at the Apostles' feet, (***he gave all to the Church***).

   Note: *Under the Old Testament Levites received the **Offering** and here in the New Testament a Levite gave the **Offering**. From Acts 4:36-37 it is no more Levitical Order but Apostolic Order.*

In the Early Church the standard of ***Giving*** was not fixed. The practice of ***Giving*** 10% (***Tithe***) was only a guideline. The ***10% (Law)*** is the level of a Pharisee and ***more than 10% (Grace)*** is the level of a Christian. Jesus Christ admonishes us to let our righteousness exceed that of the Pharisee in doing what God requires (Matt.5:20). Therefore it behoves on Christians to give more than 10% progressively (increasing your tithe gradually) to support God's work.

DISCUSSIONS:

1. Mention at least two characteristics portrayed by the Early Church according to Acts 4:32-35.
2. How did they give to support the ministry of the church?
3. Compare your answer to what pertains in your congregation.
4. Under the Grace, what percentage is expected form a Christian? Explain

FACTS TO REMEMBER

The people of the Early Church were one in mind and in spirit. They gave willingly and whole heartedly to support the ministry of the church. Our righteousness must exceed that of the Pharisee in doing what God requires. We must give progressively to support God work.

Lesson 14 | Who Should Give Tithe And Offerings?

READ

2 Cor. 9:7 "You should each give, then, as you have decided, not with regret or out of a sense of duty; for God loves the one who gives gladly."

STUDY

The Lord holds us accountable for the special responsibility of managing and taking care of the things He has given us.

1. **MATURED CHRISTIANS**

Generous ***Giving*** is a proof of our love, faith and maturity

2 Cor. 9:13 "And because of the proof which this service of yours brings, many will give glory to God for your loyalty to the gospel of Christ, which you profess, and for your generosity in sharing with them and everyone else".

2. **THOSE WHO RECEIVED GENEROUSLY FROM BELIEVERS**

This will cause the receivers to give thanks to God.

2 Cor. 9:11 "He will always make you rich enough to be generous at all times, so that many will thank God for your gifts which they receive from us."

3. **ANY ONE WHO HAS RECEIVED BLESSINGS FROM GOD**

Christians give according to how God has blessed them.

1 Chron. 29:14 "Yet my people and I cannot really give you anything, because everything is a gift from you, and we have only given back what is yours already."

4. **THOSE WHO WORK IN THE CHURCH**

Church Workers must give to support God's work.

Num.18: 26 to say to the Levites: "When you receive from the Israelites the tithe that the LORD gives you as your possession, you must present a tenth of it as a special contribution to the LORD".

1. **THE POOR**

The Macedonian Christians were in great poverty, yet they gave liberally. They had learnt obedience in giving. The poor need to give because they need God's blessing to break the curse of poverty.

2 Cor. 8:2 "They have been severely tested by the troubles they went through; but their joy was so great that they were extremely generous in their giving, even though they are very poor."

DISCUSSIONS:

Name two groups of people who should pay ***Tithe*** and ***Offerings***?

2. Discuss 2 Cor. 8:2, how do you understand the poor paying tithe and offerings?
3. What breaks the curse of poverty?
4. Who are Church workers; are they to pay ***Tithe*** and ***Offerings***? Why?

FACTS TO REMEMBER

God holds us accountable for all that we have. Each individual who has received God's blessing is expected to pay tithe and offering to support the work of God.

Lesson 15 | Purpose Of Giving (Tithing And Offering)

READ

Pro 3:9-10 – "Honor the LORD by making him an offering from the best of all that your land produces. If you do, your barns will be filled with grain, and you will have too much wine to store it all.

b. ***Num. 18:26 – "The Lord required a special tithe for the priests and all workers of God from the offerings given by those to whom they minister or serve".***

c. ***Mal 3:10a "Bring the full amount of your tithes to the Temple, so that there will be plenty of food there."***

STUDY

Christians are owner-stewards which means that they own whatever God has given them and at the same time taking care of it for God.

1. **To enable the growth of God's work –** (Evangelism, Nurture and Church Growth)
2. **To support the poor, helpless, hungry and the needy in the church (God's family or believers) and the community.**
   a. Acts 24:17 – *"After an absence of several years, I came to Jerusalem to bring my people gifts for the poor and to present offerings."* NIV
   b. Lev. 19:10 – *"Do not go back through your vineyard to gather the grapes that were missed or to pick up the grapes that have fallen; leave them for poor people and foreigners. I am the LORD your God".*
   c. Rom. 15:26 – *"For the churches in Macedonia and Achaia have freely decided to give an offering to help the poor among God's people in Jerusalem."*
3. **To support the Priests, Ministers, Teachers, Church Workers, staff, services and worships, projects, church support teams and leaders of the church.**
   a. Roman 12:13 – *"Contribute to the needs of the saints and seek to show hospitality" ESV*
   b. Gal. 6:6 – *"If you are being taught the Christian message, you should share all the good things you have with your teacher".*

1 Cor. 9:14 – "*In the same way, the Lord has ordered that those who preach the gospel should get their living from it*".

d. 1 Tim 5:18 – *For the Scripture says, "Do not muzzle the ox while it is treading out the grain," and "The worker deserves his wages." NIV*

DISCUSSIONS:

How do you understand Rom 15:26?

2. Mention three purposes for paying tithe and offering.
3. How can the projects of the church be supported?
4. In what way can you support the ministry of your Church?

FACTS TO REMEMBER

God expects all Christians to support the ministry – (*evangelism, projects, the needy etc.*) of the church through ***Giving*** (***Tithes And Offerings***). We give to the Church in order to fulfil God's purpose and command.

Lesson 16 | How To Calculate The Amount To Give (Practice And Standard)

In the Early Church the standard of giving was not fixed. The practice of giving 10% (tithe) was only a guideline. The ***10% (Law)*** is the level of a Pharisee and ***more than 10% (Grace)*** is the level of a Christian. Jesus Christ admonishes us to let our righteousness exceed that of the Pharisee in doing what God requires (Matt.5:20). Therefore it behoves on Christians to give more than 10% progressively (increasing your tithe gradually) to support God's work.
(Ref. Lesson 13)

READINGS AND STUDY

Before the LAW 10% (Melchizedek Order)

a. Gen.14:20b – "Then Abram gave him a tenth of everything." NIV

b. Gen. 28:22 – "This memorial stone which I have set up will be the place where you are worshiped, and I will give you a tenth of everything you give me."

c. Heb. 7:1-2,6 – For this Melchizedek, king of Salem, priest of the Most High God, met Abraham returning from the slaughter of the kings and blessed him, 2 and to him Abraham apportioned a tenth part of everything. He is first, by translation of his name, king of righteousness, and then he is also king of Salem, that is, king of peace... But this man who does not have his descent from them received tithes from Abraham and blessed him who had the promises." ESV

2. **Under the LAW 10%** (Levitical Order)

Lev. 27:30 – "A tithe of everything from the land, whether grain from the soil or fruit from the trees, belongs to the Lord; it is holy to the Lord." NIV

3. **New Testament – more than 10%** (Apostolic Order)

Luke11:42 – "How terrible for you Pharisees! You give to God one tenth of the seasoning herbs, such as mint and rue and all the other herbs, but you neglect justice and love for God. ***These you should practice,***

without neglecting the others."

4. **Pattern for calculating – set a priority**

   a. *First fruits*

   - *Exo. 34: 26a – "Bring the best of the firstfruits of your soil to the house of the Lord your God." NIV*
   - *Pro.3:9 – "Honor the Lord with your wealth and with the firstfruits of all your produce." ESV*

   In proportion to your earning

   - *1 Cor. 16:2 – Every Sunday each of you must put aside some money, in proportion to what you have earned, and save it up, so that there will be no need to collect money when I come."*

5. **Promptly**

   a. *Exodus 22:29 – "You shall not delay to offer from the fullness of your harvest and from the outflow of your presses. The firstborn of your sons you shall give to me." ESV*

   b. *Deut. 23:21 – "If you make a vow to the Lord your God, you shall not delay fulfilling it, for the Lord your God will surely require it of you, and you will be guilty of sin." ESV*

   c. *Eccl. 5:4 – "So when you make a promise to God, keep it as quickly as possible. He has no use for a fool. Do what you promise to do."*

6. **Periodically**

   a. *Deut. 14:22 – "You shall tithe all the yield of your seed that comes from the field year by year." ESV*

   b. *1 Cor.16:2 – "On the first day of every week, each of you is to put something aside and store it up, as he may prosper, so that there will be no collecting when I come." ESV*

7. **Personal**

   a. *Deut. 16:17, "Each of you must bring a gift in proportion to the way the Lord your God has blessed you." NIV*

   b. *Acts 9:36 – "In Joppa there was a disciple named Tabitha (which, when translated, is Dorcas), who was always doing good and helping the poor." NIV*

8. **With God's blessing the 90% can purchase more than the**

100% would without His blessing.

Lev. 27:32 "One of every ten domestic animals belongs to the LORD. When the animals are counted, every tenth one belongs to the LORD".

9. **Look beyond your regular earnings.**

   2 Chron. 31:5 "As soon as the order was given, the people of Israel brought gifts of their finest grain, wine, olive oil, honey, and other farm produce, and they also brought the tithes of everything they had".

   b. 2 Chron. 31:6 "All the people who lived in the cities of Judah brought tithes of their cattle and sheep, and they also brought large quantities of gifts which they dedicated to the LORD their God."

10. **When you borrow the 10%, add 20% (that is paying back the 10% plus 20% interest).**

    a. Lev. 27:13 "If you wish to buy it back, you must pay the price plus an additional 20 percent."
    b. Lev. 27:31 "If you wish to buy any of it back, you must pay the standard price plus an additional 20 percent."

DISCUSSIONS:

How do you calculate your ***Tithe***? Discuss

2. How can the percentage of 10% be a guide and a standard of ***Giving?***
3. How is God not a Tax-Collector
4. Can I give beyond my regular income? How?

FACTS TO REMEMBER

Know the purpose, the needs, projects, activities and ministries of your Church. Know how much you earn or receive and that will help you to determine how much you will give. Sometimes **Give** more and Use the percentage as a guide and a standard. God loves a cheerful ***Giver;*** He is not a Tax Collector but a Heavenly Father. ***Believe that the 90% you have left after Tithing has God's blessing.***

Lesson 17 | Where To Pay Your Tithe And Offerings

READ

Malachi 3:10 "Bring the full amount of your tithes to the Temple, so that there will be plenty of food there. Put me to the test and you will see that I will open the windows of heaven and pour out on you in abundance all kinds of good things."

STUDY

1. ***Send it to the right place, (where receivers do so, on behalf of the Church).***
   Send your ***Tithe and Offerings*** to the place you trust. To the church which is under proper stewardship of the money received.
2. ***Where God will choose or direct- (Receivers are only receivers but not Users).***
   Deut. 14:23 "Then go to the one place where the LORD your God has chosen to be worshiped; and there in his presence eat the tithes of your grain, wine, and olive oil, and the first- born of your cattle and sheep. Do this so that you may learn to honor the LORD your God always."
3. ***Store house of the Lord or the Church treasurer (where proper financial arrangements are in place)***
   a. Neh. 13:12 "Then all the people of Israel again started bringing to the Temple storerooms ...."
   b. Neh. 10:38b "... the Levites are to take to the Temple storerooms one-tenth of all the tithes they collect."

4. ***Your place of worship (where receivers are accountable).***
   Deut. 14:24-25 "If the place of worship is too far from your home for you to carry there the tithe of the produce that the LORD has blessed you with, then do this: Sell your produce and take the money with you to the one place of worship."

DISCUSSIONS:

Where do you send your ***Tithe and Offerings*** why?

2. How do you understand "*where God has chosen*"?
3. What is the "*store house of the Lord*" in the present church system?
4. If you live far away, what do you do with your ***Tithe and Offerings***? Discuss the current electronic banking and money transfer facilities available.

FACTS TO REMEMBER

Send your ***Tithes and Offerings*** to the house of the Lord or the church treasury. Pay at where the Lord directs and the receiver is accountable. Every Church must ensure that there are well structured or proper financial arrangements in place to receive and account for the ***Tithes and Offerings.***

Lesson 18 | To Whom Should You Pay Tithe And Offerings

READ

a. Numbers 18:26 "to say to the Levites: "When you receive from the Israelites the tithe that the Lord gives you as your possession, you must present a tenth of it as a special contribution to the Lord"

b. Acts 4:35, 37 – "And laid it at the apostles' feet, and it was distributed to each as any had need... sold a field that belonged to him and brought the money and laid it at the apostles' feet." ESV

STUDY

Tithes and ***Offerings*** are institutional acts which demands accountability. It should always be received by the representative of God and such a representative should have a character of God, which is righteousness. The fact that the representative receives the ***Tithe*** *and* ***Offering*** does not mean they belong to him or her. The ***Tithes*** and ***Offerings*** are received on behalf of the church. During the Old Testament time, it was given to the Levites in the Temple *(Neh.10:37b)*. Currently, each church's institution has a financial arrangement or appointed finance committee which receive the ***Tithes*** and ***Offerings*** on behalf of the church. The persons responsible for the financial arrangement or committee must bear in mind that they are receivers and not users. Also they are accountable to God and the church.

1. **To the Church**
   a. 2 Chron. 31:11-12a – "On the king's orders they prepared storerooms in the Temple area and put all the gifts and tithes in them for safekeeping...."
   b. Neh. 13:12 – "Then all the people of Israel again started bringing to the Temple storerooms their tithes of grain, wine, and olive oil."

2. **To Church workers and God's people**
   Deut. 14:29 – "This food is for the Levites, since they own no property... Do this, and the LORD your God will bless you in everything you do."

3. **To the needy – foreigners, orphans and the widows in the community.**

    Deut. 26:12b "… the foreigners, the orphans, and the widows, so that in every community they will have all they need to eat. When you have done this."

    b. Acts 20:35 – "In everything I did, I showed you that by this kind of hard work we must help the weak, remembering the words the Lord Jesus himself said: 'It is more blessed to give than to receive." NIV

    c. Ps 9:18 – "But the needy will not always be forgotten, nor the hope of the afflicted ever perish." NIV

4. **An arrangement of a local Congregation or denomination, that is Biblical and ethical.**

5. **An individual arrangement that will enable him or her to fulfil the requirement of an owner-steward or owner- manager of God's resources.**

DISCUSSIONS:

1. According to 2 Chron. 31:11-12, why did they prepare the storeroom in the temple?
2. The Bible says we should bring the full amount of our tithe and offering to where?

    Does your Church have any arrangements for the payment of tithes and offerings? Explain your answer.
4. What arrangements are there in your church to support the needy – poor, orphans, widows etc.?

FACTS TO REMEMBER

Tithes and ***Offerings*** are institutional acts which demands accountability. People responsible for receiving ***Tithes*** and ***Offerings*** are mere receivers and not users. They are accountable to God and the church.

Lesson 19 | What Happens When You Fail To Pay Tithe And Offerings

READ

Malachi 3:8 – 9 "I ask you, is it right for a person to cheat God? Of course not, yet you are cheating me. 'How?' you ask. In the matter of tithes and offerings. A curse is on all of you because the whole nation is cheating me."

STUDY:

1. **You rob God**

   Everything we have is from God. So when we refuse to return to Him a part of what He has given us we rob Him. The people of Malachi's day ignored God's command to give a tenth of their income to His temple; God called this robbing.

2. **You become ungrateful**

   Do you selfishly want to keep 100% of what God gives you, or are you willing to return at least 10% to help advance His Kingdom? When you do not return the 10%, you are ungrateful to God.

3. **You cheat God**

   Mal 3: 8 – "I ask you, is it right for a person to cheat God? Of course not, yet you are cheating me. How, you ask? In the matter of tithes and offerings."

4. **You come under a curse**

   a. Mal 3:9 - "A curse is on all of you because the whole nation is cheating me".

   b. Deut. 28:38-46 (the leader should read portions that may relate to point four)

5. **You spend what belongs to God.**

   Lev. 27:30 - "One tenth of all the produce of the land, whether grain or fruit, belongs to the LORD".

DISCUSSIONS:

1. What happens when one fails to pay his or her tithe and offerings? How do you understand Mal 3:10?
3. Put these verses in a word or two: Mal.3:9; Lev. 27:30
4. Why do some Christian fail to give tithe and offerings?

FACTS TO REMEMBER

Failure to pay ***Tithe*** and ***Offerings*** is total disobedience to God. This may attract a curse from God. God has not changed and His principles are for all times.

Lesson 20 | God Loves A Cheerful Giver (Tithe and Offerings)

READ

2 Cor.9:7-12 - "Each man should give what he has decided in his heart to give, not reluctantly or under compulsion, for God loves a cheerful giver. 8 And God is able to make all grace abound to you, so that in all things at all times, having all that you need, you will abound in every good work. 9 As it is written: "He has scattered abroad his gifts to the poor; his righteousness endures forever." 10 Now he who supplies seed to the sower and bread for food will also supply and increase your store of seed and will enlarge the harvest of your righteousness. 11 You will be made rich in every way so that you can be generous on every occasion, and through us your generosity will result in thanksgiving to God. 12 This service that you perform is not only supplying the needs of God's people but is also overflowing in many expressions of thanks to God." NIV

b. ***Luke 21:2-4 – "He also saw a poor widow put in two very small copper coins. 3 "I tell you the truth," he said, "this poor widow has put in more than all the others. 4 All these people gave their gifts out of their wealth; but she out of her poverty put in all she had to live on." NIV***

STUDY

The Bible teaches us that, we are to give ***willingly*** and ***cheerfully,*** from a spirit of ***generosity***. We must decide what we want to give in our hearts and plan towards it without compulsion. This is because whoever sows sparingly will also reap sparingly, and whoever sows generously will also reap generously. God rewards us according to what is left after we give and also the motive and the heart with which we give. The principles regarding ***Giving – Tithes*** and **Offering** are intended to encourage inward attitudes and outward actions. If a person gives grudgingly, he shows that he has a stingy heart; God wants us to be cheerful givers. When we give cheerfully and wholeheartedly, God promised to pour out His blessings upon us until we need no more and our barns will be full.

Remember, *"For if the willingness is there, the gift is acceptable according to what one has, not according to what he does not have." 2 Cor. 8:12 NIV*

DISCUSSIONS:

1. Who is a cheerful giver? Explain your answer
   How can giving meet God's special promise?
3. How can giving show a person's faith?
4. In what way do we give to attract God's approval?
5. How do you understand 2 Cor. 8:12?

FACTS TO REMEMBER

Decide in your heart what you want to give. Give willingly and cheerfully and not reluctantly or under any compulsion. Giving willingly and wholeheartedly unlocks God promise of abundant blessings. *"For if the willingness is there, the gift is acceptable according to what one has, not according to what he does not have." 2 Cor. 8:12 NIV*

Summary

Giving – Tithing and Offerings do not buy God's blessings, but they do release His blessing upon our lives. *Mal 3:10 "Bring the full amount of your tithes to the Temple, so that there will be plenty of food there. Put me to the test and you will see that I will open the windows of heaven and pour out on you in abundance all kinds of good things".*

The Bible teaches us that we control the flow or the amount of God's blessings and provision to our need. It is a privilege of those who choose to exercise their faith to give. To those who give, God makes a special promise.

If we give spoonful to the Lord, He will pick up the same spoon we used and use it to spoon out what we ask for. ***Tithing and Offerings*** express our faith in God in the most practical way. They also break the curse of poverty and bring God's blessings upon us.

Remember that the person who plants few seeds will have a small crop and the one who plants many seeds will have a large crop. God is able to give you more than you need, so that you will always have all you need for yourselves and more than enough for every good cause. As the scripture says, *"He gives generously to the needy; His kindness lasts forever."* And God, who supplies seed for the sower and bread to eat, will also supply you with all the seed you need and will make it grow and produce a rich harvest from your generosity.

If you are a Christian give, for giving is a mark of your Christianity. Let your highest financial donation go to the Church and it should be your number one priority.

May God Bless You For Being A Cheerful Giver, Amen.

About The Author

REV. PETER KOFI NYARKOH is an ordained Minister of the Presbyterian Church of Ghana. He has a teaching Ministry that is reaching the nation of Ghana and touching the world. He is a Specialist in Evangelism and Church Growth. Early in his ministry, as he studied God's word in depth, opportunities began to open for him to conduct training courses, seminars, revival programmes, miracle services and open air programmes throughout the country.

Today, Rev. Nyarkoh is answering God's call to awaken the sleeping giants, Christian Pastors, Christian Lay Persons and all those engaged in the ministry to rescue the perishing and care for the dying, with the Bible in a simple and practical way. He is revealing the authority of God's word as a creative power and bringing the life of God into the lives of people, all over the country and outside Ghana.

He has served his Church as a full time minister, in various capacities since 1984 to date. He was a second Minister at Abetifi-Kwahu, Presbyterian Church of Ghana from 1984 – 1986. He then served as a Sub-District Minister at Asawase – Kumasi for five years (1986 – 1991). He took charge of Presbyterian Church of Ghana, Suhum - District from 1992 – 1993, as a District Minister. He also served as District Minster in charge of Presbyterian Church of Ghana, Dorma Ahenkro District from 1995-1998.

Rev. Peter Kofi Nyarkoh was elected as the Kwahu Presbytery Chairperson, Synod Committee Member and General Assembly Council Member in 1998 and served till 2003. Within that period, he also served as a General Assembly Council Standing Committee member. After his term of office, he was transferred to the German District of Presbyterian Church of Ghana from 2003 – 2007, where he took charge of PCG Germany District (*Hamburg, Berlin, Stuggart, Frankfurt, Dusseldorf and Bremen – PCG congregations*). At the same time, he also served as a Supporting Minister for PCG Italy and London between 2004 and 2007 and a supervising Minister for PCG Amsterdam from 2005-2007. He came back to Ghana and became the District Minister in charge of PCG, Bantama District from 2007- 2010 and a Minister in charge of PCG, Ebenezer Congregation, Mamprobi-Accra from 2010-2012.

He was sent as a Visiting Minister to PCG North America OMF District, stationed at Irvington, New Jersey USA from January-May, 2012. He then became the Minister in charge of PCG, Irvington Congregation, New Jersey, USA, from 2012-2014; District Minister in charge of New Jersey District, New Jersey - USA from 2013-2014.

In 2014, he was elected as the Presbytery Chairperson for the New Europe Presbytery created by the Presbyterian Church of Ghana. During his term as a Chairperson he also served as the District Minister in Charge of PCG South London District, London UK from 2014-2017; Minister in charge PCG, Trinity Congregation, South Lee, London UK from 2014-2017; when he was detached in order to concentrate on his work as a detached (fulltime) Chairperson. During his term as Chairperson of PCG Europe Presbytery he worked across nine nations namely – United Kingdom, Germany, Italy, Spain, France, Netherlands, Belgium, Demark and Norway).

Other areas in which Rev. Nyarkoh made use of his God-given abilities and special gifts to serve his church were: Youth Pastor for Kumasi District – 1987 to 1989; Director of Evangelism and Lay Training Committee – Northern Sector of the Presbyterian Church Ghana – 1988 to1991, Secretary for Ghana Evangelism Committee – 1991 to 1992. Director of Evangelism and Lay Training Committee – Southern Sector –1991 to 1993.General Secretary of Evangelism and Lay Training (ELTC), 1991 to 1993. Tutor and Deputy Director RTC (Ramseyer Training Centre) from 1993-1995; Area Board Chairman-Kwahu Presbytery Health Services – 1998 to 2003. Board Member, Presbyterian Senior Secondary Schools (Nkwatia and Abetifi) and Presbyterian College of Education, Abetifi – 1998 to 2003. Rev Nyarkoh became the National Chaplain for Men's Ministry - PCG and chairperson for Committee on Global Mission-PCG, from 2009-2012.

REV. PETER KOFI NYAKROH has also written more than 14 bestselling books including Presbyter's Handbook, Bible Study Made Simple, Preaching Skills and Pulpit Manners, Increasing Church Membership and Marriage Counselling Handbook among others.

Currently, he is the District Minister of Santasi District of the Presbyterian Church of Ghana. He is married to MRS. GRACE NYARKOH and a father of four children with six grandchildren.

www.ingramcontent.com/pod-product-compliance
Ingram Content Group UK Ltd.
Pitfield, Milton Keynes, MK11 3LW, UK
UKHW022009190726
13853UKWH00004B/1832

9 789988 535797